How to get re

Write a letter
to Santa

Decorate
yourself with
baubles

Sing some nice
Christmas songs

Wear fancy trousers to
keep your bottom
warm on Christmas Eve

For
Colin Williams and Michelle Forde

HODDER CHILDREN'S BOOKS
First published in Great Britain in 2016 by Hodder and Stoughton
This edition published in 2017

1 3 5 7 9 10 8 6 4 2

Text and illustrations copyright © Alex T. Smith, 2016

The moral rights of the author have been asserted.

A CIP catalogue record for this book is available from the British Library.

ISBN: 978 1 444 919615

Design by Alison Still

Printed and bound in Spain by Unigraf

The paper and board used in this book are made from wood from
responsible sources.

Hodder Children's Books
A division of Hachette Children's Group
Carmelite House, 50 Victoria Embankment, London EC4Y 0DZ
www.hachettechildrens.co.uk
An Hachette UK Company
www.hachette.co.uk

SANTA CLAUDE

ALEX T. SMITH

In a rather festive house on
Waggy Avenue, there lives a dog.
A small, plump dog.

Claude

A jaunty jumper

Sir Bobblysock

A small, plump dog called Claude,
who wears a jaunty jumper and a
very snazzy beret.

4

Claude lives with Mr and Mrs
Shinyshoes and his best friend
Sir Bobblysock, who is a very
bobbly sock.

Whenever Mr and Mrs Shinyshoes
are out of the house, Claude
and Sir Bobblysock go on an
adventure. What adventure will
they have today?

'Twas the night before
Christmas and Mr and Mrs
Shinyshoes were off to a party
in the city. They were looking
terribly glamorous.

'See you later!' said Mrs
Shinyshoes, slipping into
her slingbacks.

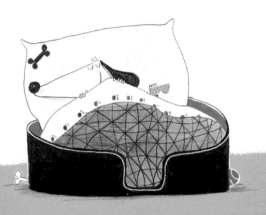

'We'll be back at midnight!'
cried Mr Shinyshoes,
straightening his dickie bow.

Then they both blew kisses
towards Claude, who was fast
asleep, and clattered out of the
front door into the snowy night.

7

Claude waited a few moments…
listening…

When he was absolutely sure that
he and Sir Bobblysock were alone
in the house, he pinged open his
eyes and sat up in bed.

Then he flung everything
out of his beret and had a
jolly good root around in it.

Gosh!
  He was
    ever so
      excited!

'AHA!' he cried eventually (in his Outdoor Voice), and from the depths of his hat he produced an enormous hardback book.

He'd been really looking forward to reading it since his friend and favourite police person, PC Anne Cuffs, had presented it to him with his very own pair of special police handcuffs to say thank you for rescuing her earlier that afternoon.

Claude and Sir Bobblysock had discovered her dangling from her utility belt, her legs waggling and the keys on her key ring jangling. She'd been decorating the police station when the ladder slipped and left her hanging in midair.

Claude had quickly righted the ladder and spent the day helping Anne with the tree. Sir Bobblysock thought he looked lovely draped in tinsel, but that's another story...

13

PC Anne Cuffs wasn't the only person Claude and Sir Bobblysock had helped that week.

They'd fed the pigeons.

They'd helped Beverly Clematis, the florist, make holly wreaths for people's knockers.

They'd sung some lovely Christmas songs with their friend Carol Singer's choir…

(Claude didn't really know the proper words so he just made them up.)

Deck the halls and jingle your bells!

Here comes the Christmas hippo! She's wearing a lovely hat!

And they'd been kept very busy indeed at the post office! Percy Package, the postman, had been in a real tizz with all the letters for Santa until Claude and Sir Bobblysock had bustled in to help.

Percy helped the children stick stamps on their letters.

Claude helped put their letters in great big sacks.

Sir Bobblysock helped by sitting on a swizzly office chair with a clipboard and making sure everyone did everything properly.

At the end of the day there was just time for Claude to write his own letter to Santa, which he did in his best handwriting. Then he stuck a stamp on it and popped it in the sack with the others. He wasn't sure what he really wanted for Christmas, so he asked for a surprise!

Dear Santa,
Please can I have a surprise for Christmas.
Claude x

Santa Claus
The North Pole

'I wonder what would happen if I stuck a stamp on myself and sat in one of these bags?' thought Claude.

Thankfully Percy spotted Claude just as the bags were being loaded into a big van to be sent to the North Pole.

Back in his cosy bed on Christmas Eve Claude snuggled down in the darkness to read his new Cops and Robbers book. Then he rummaged around in his beret once again and took out his special reading lamp, and switched it on.

21

It was a clever head torch – just perfect for reading when you had a big, heavy book and your paws were really rather on the small side. And it left your hands free for dunking biscuits in a nice cup of tea, which is never a bad thing.

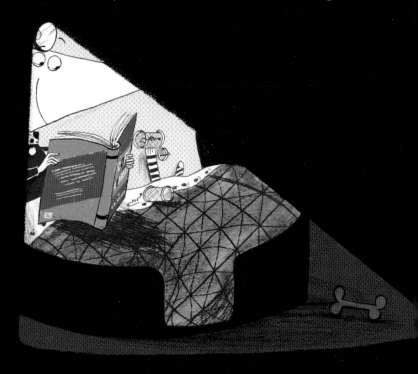

Sir Bobblysock busied himself carefully jabbing hairpins into his curlers to keep them nicely in place and Claude settled down to read his book.

Goodness!
It was exciting!

Claude flicked through the pages to show Sir Bobblysock – there were dastardly robbers, brave police officers, thrilling car chases and –

THUD!

'What was that?' hissed Claude in the darkness. He cocked his ears to listen.

It sounded like FOOTSTEPS!

'I think someone is IN our house!' hissed Claude. His eyes grew big and wide like saucers and his bottom wiggled his tail about like billy-o – half with nerves and half with giddy excitement.

Sir Bobblysock was all a-quiver too. His specs were steamed up and his curlers were askew.

THUD! THUD! THUD!
THUD! THUD!
THUD!

Whoever could it be? Who on earth could have snuck into their house on Christmas Eve?

Claude suddenly gasped! He knew exactly who it was...

A BURGLAR! A burglar! Right here on Waggy Avenue!

His eyebrows started to waggle with excitement. This was absolutely the start of an adventure and his big chance to catch a burglar RED-HANDED just like a police officer!

'Claude, you are a hero!'

Cor! he thought.
Wouldn't his friend
PC Anne Cuffs be
proud of him!

27

Claude fished around in his beret
for his handcuffs, switched off his
head torch and tiptoed ever so
quietly to the door.

Sir Bobblysock really wanted to
supervise from the safety and
comfort of his bed, with his head
under the covers, but thought
he'd better help out.

'After three!' whispered Claude
with his hand on the door.

'One... Two... Three...'

CRASH!

Claude thundered into the pitch-black living room. He barged into the burglar's knees and pushed him to the ground. Then he clapped the handcuffs around his wrists and locked them –

CLINK!

– around the arm of a chair.

Sir Bobblysock then hoofed in and bopped the intruder on the nose with a rolled-up magazine for good measure.

'HA HA!'

cried Claude triumphantly. 'Now let's see what you look like, you naughty robber!'

And he switched on the lights.

Uh… oh…

It wasn't a burglar handcuffed to
the armchair…

It was…

'SANTA!?'

gasped Claude.

Claude wondered if someone had turned the radiators up because he suddenly felt a bit hot under the head torch. Sir Bobblysock had one of his tropical moments.

Claude fussed with the hem of his jumper and quickly explained to Santa how he thought he might actually have been a robber.

'I'm very sorry…' he said in a quiet voice.

'Don't you worry!' said Santa, chuckling. 'Now would you mind awfully letting me out of these cuffs? I've got a jolly busy night tonight. Have you got the key handy?'

Claude blinked for a moment.
A key... Yes, there ought to be a
tiny key for those handcuffs, but
where was it?

Quickly Claude found his beret
and emptied the contents out again
onto the carpet. Then he looked in
all the nooks and crannies.

36

Finally, he peered under his
jumper and inside his shoes.

Sir Bobblysock went to check
if the key was in the pocket of
his quilted bed jacket or in his
sewing box, but it wasn't.

In fact, it wasn't
ANYWHERE!

'Oh dear! Oh dear!' sighed Santa. 'Whatever will we do? I have all these presents to deliver before the sun comes up…'

Claude ran his foot around in a circle. This WAS a problem! And he'd caused it… If only he could help in some way…

Suddenly he had an idea!

'We can do it!'

he shouted. 'We have to be back by midnight, but I'm sure we'll get them all delivered by then!'

Santa wasn't very sure at all, but didn't really know what else he could do.

'It's jolly cold flying about in the sky on a sleigh,' he said. 'Do you have a coat?'

Claude nodded and wiggled into his toasty anorak.

'You might need something to keep your botty warm too...' said Santa. 'Why don't you borrow my lovely trousers?'

They were a **bit** big but Claude tucked his anorak into them and pulled the belt buckle tight.

'Finally,' said Santa, 'you'll need this,' and he popped his special hat on top of Claude's beret. Claude looked very smart. Sir Bobblysock admired his pompom.

42

'Now, to get up and down
the chimneys easily,' Santa
continued, 'you must remember
to tap the side of your nose.
Then you'll whizz up and down
no problem!'

Claude nodded.

Sir Bobblysock carefully wrapped
a headscarf over his curlers,
Claude tapped the side of his
nose, and just as Santa had
said the two friends whipped
magically up the chimney.

On the roof was a very handsome
reindeer and a beautiful sleigh.
On the back of it, in the biggest
bag Claude had ever seen, were
hundreds and hundreds and
HUNDREDS of presents.

It was going to be a jolly busy night.

Claude and Sir Bobblysock
hopped into the driver's seat
and with a flick of the reins
they were off. Whoooooooosh!
Up into the sky on their very
                    important
                        mission!

The first house was a bit tricky. Claude forgot to do Santa's special nose-tapping trick,

so ended up hurling himself down the chimney with Sir Bobblysock rattling along behind him.

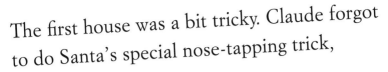

The two friends exploded into the living room in a great big cloud of soot and dust!

Claude quickly piled up the presents under the tree, put the cookies addressed to Santa Claus under his beret for later and skedaddled back up the chimney.

Sir Bobblysock hoped one of the presents was a vacuum cleaner to clean up all that mess.

In the next house, Claude got
his foot caught up in a string of
fairy lights on the way back up
onto the roof.

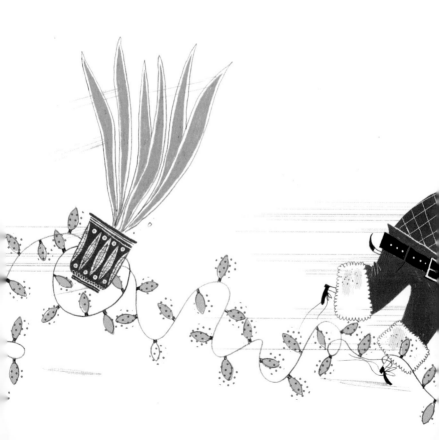

In the third, he knocked over the Christmas tree and in the fourth he startled someone's pet parrot.

'SQUARK!' went the parrot.

'GREAT GLITTERY BAUBLES!' cried Claude in surprise.

'GREAT GLITTERY BAUBLES!' shouted the parrot, who liked to repeat things.

'Shh! You silly sausage!' hissed Claude.

'SHH, YOU SILLY SAUSAGE!' yelled the parrot.

Sir Bobblysock said that that was the problem with parrots – there was no talking to them – so he and Claude whooshed back up the chimney leaving the parrot all alone shouting about sausages and baubles…

At the next house there was a
problem. It didn't have a chimney.

How on earth are we going to
get in? wondered Claude, as
he parked the reindeer in the
front garden.

The two friends checked the
doors and windows, but they
were all locked shut.
Then Sir
Bobblysock
spotted
something –

999
LETSBY
AVE.

It was a cat flap.

'Well done, Sir Bobblysock!' hollered Claude. He smoothed down his ears, sucked in his tummy and squeezed through the little hole with an armful of presents.

Sir Bobblysock followed behind very carefully so as to not upset his curlers and headscarf.

The two friends put out the
presents under the tree and
Sir Bobblysock excelled himself
at titivating all the bows and
parcel tags.

'Super dooper!' said Claude.
'We're really getting the
hang of this now!' He
stepped back to admire
their work and…

Over went a plate of biscuits and a glass of milk –

SMASH!

– onto the floor!

Sir Bobblysock was just thinking that the tissue he'd left tucked up the arm of his cardigan at home would be very useful just now when from upstairs there came a voice.

'Hello? Is someone there?' it called, and footsteps sounded on the staircase.

'YIKES!'

yelped Claude. 'Quick! No one
is meant to see us!' And the two
pals ran for the cat flap.

Sir Bobblysock hopped out easily,
but when Claude dived through –
oh dear! – he forgot to suck in
his tummy and he got well and
truly WEDGED.

'Help, Sir Bobblysock!' he cried.
'Quickly, before I'm caught!'

But it was too late!

Behind Claude there were
footsteps. Then the door he
was wedged in swung open and
standing in front of him was

PC Anne Cuffs.
In her nightie.
With her hands on her hips.

'Claude! What on earth are you
doing dressed as Santa Claus and
stuck in my cat flap in the middle
of the night?'

She gently pushed Claude's
bottom through the cat flap and
he told her all about what had
happened.

He explained how he'd accidentally handcuffed Santa Claus to the armchair at home, how he'd lost the key and how he'd borrowed Santa's special warm trousers and hat so that he and Sir Bobblysock could go out to deliver presents.

'But,' he said finally, 'we've only delivered parcels to five houses and we need to get them all done before Mr and Mrs Shinyshoes come back home at midnight OR we need to think of a way to get Santa out of those handcuffs…'

He sighed and Sir Bobblysock
did too, partly to copy Claude,
but mainly because he wanted to
be in the warm again and could
hear his bed jacket calling.

sigh...

'Midnight?!' exclaimed Anne Cuffs. 'But, look! It's almost midnight now!' She showed them the time on her watch. Ten minutes to go!

'Oh no!'
cried Claude, panicking.

'WHAT WILL WE DO?'

'Don't worry!' said Anne.
'I'll come with you and help!
I've ALWAYS wanted to meet
Santa. Together we'll think of
something!'

And so she and Claude gambolled over the front of the sleigh like the police did over their cars in Claude's book. Sir Bobblysock thought about doing the same but his ankles were stiff with cold and he was still terrifically worried about his curlers staying in place so he gently climbed in and settled himself under the knee blanket.

WHIZZ!

Through the snowy air went the sleigh and a few minutes later, Claude, Anne and Sir Bobblysock crashed onto the roof of 112 Waggy Avenue and shimmied down the chimney with a tap of Claude's nose.

Santa was ever so glad to see them.

'I've tried everything to wiggle
my hands free,' he said, 'but they
won't budge!'

'Don't worry!' said Claude. 'We'll
save you! Won't we?'

And he looked over at Anne Cuffs,
but she was so excited
to see Santa that she just stood
there with her mouth open.

Claude took her special
key ring to see if any of the
keys would unlock the
handcuffs.

72

But none of them did!

'The lock is too small!' he cried.

Claude rummaged around in
his beret and brought out a saw.
He could try sawing through the
handcuffs.

'No!' cried
Santa and Anne Cuffs.

The clock on the mantelpiece
struck midnight.

'Oh no! This is a disaster!'
said Claude, doing a funny little
panicky dance on the carpet.
'Mr and Mrs Shinyshoes will
be back any second!'

Indeed, at that very moment,
it sounded like a taxi was slowly
making its way down snowy
Waggy Avenue.

Sir Bobblysock was trembling
all over with worry. His bobbles
bobbled about, his specs were on
sideways and his curlers jangled
about under his headscarf.

'Sometimes, very naughty robbers pick the locks with something tiny…' said Anne Cuffs, 'like a hairpin or something…'

Claude's ears leapt up.

'A hairpin?!' he said. 'Would that work?'

Anne nodded.

That was it!

Claude quickly jumped across the room and with one super-speedy swipe, he swept Sir Bobblysock up from the pouffe and jammed one of the hairpins holding his curlers in place into the lock.

Then he wiggled Sir Bobblysock. And he waggled Sir Bobblysock.

'Quick!' said Claude. 'Do a jiggly little dance to help!'

But Sir Bobblysock felt shy and couldn't dance without any music so whilst Claude and Sir Bobblysock wobbled about, Santa and Anne Cuffs sang some hearty Christmas songs.

Outside, there were footsteps coming up the steps.

JANGLE!

'Oh yikes!' cried everyone, but just then the knocker on the front door started to jangle…

Deck the halls and jingle your bells! Wrap your turkey in tinsel!

The handcuffs pinged
open and Santa Claus was

FREE!!

'HOORAY!'

everyone shouted.

But Mr and Mrs Shinyshoes
were in the hall!

Claude gave Santa his hat and trousers back and he quickly bustled to the fireplace.

'Thank you!' cried Santa. 'Don't worry about all the other presents! Leave them to me!'

And he whooshed up the chimney.

'Good work, PC Claude!' said Anne Cuffs proudly. Then she saluted, hoiked up the living room window and hopped out into the night.

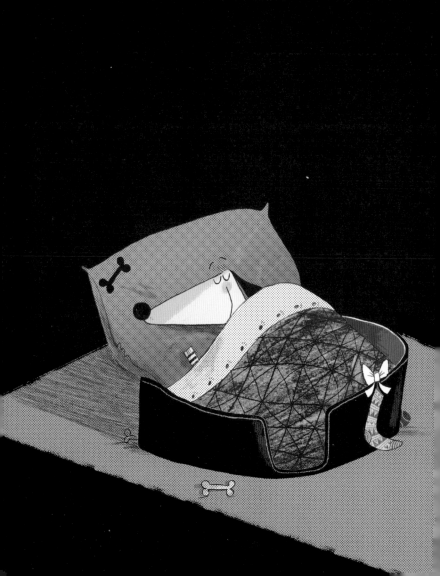

Claude and Sir Bobblysock clicked off the light, leapt across the room and dived into bed.

'Oh look…' whispered Mr Shinyshoes, popping his head around the door. 'Claude's been fast asleep all night… What a jolly good chap he is!'

When Claude woke up on Christmas morning, there were two neat little parcels addressed to him sitting on the floor beside his bed.

'Look, Santa Claus has left presents for Claude,' exclaimed Mr Shinyshoes.

Mrs Shinyshoes said, 'I wonder what they are? Let's open them!'

One was a nice letter and stuck next to it was a teeny, tiny key.

GGY AVENUE POLICE DEPT
AGGY AVENUE.
POLICE CHIEF: ANNE CUFFS

Dear Claude,

I found the missing key - I'd mistaken it for a decoration and had accidentally hung it on the police station Christmas tree. Oops! So sorry.

Love from A xxx

The second thing was a little box in which there was an ENORMOUS key ring and a little postcard with a lovely wintery scene of the North Pole on the front. On the back it said:

Thank you!
See you
next year!
Santa

xxx

POLAR POST

My friend Claude,
His bed,
The kitchen,
112 Waggy Avenue

'I wonder what they're all about?' said Mrs Shinyshoes. 'Do you think Claude knows anything about them?'

'Don't be silly!' laughed Mr Shinyshoes. 'Why would Claude need a tiny key and a gigantic key ring?'

But Claude DID know what he needed them for. And we do too, don't we?

Merry Christmas from
Claude, Sir Bobblysock
and all of your chums
on Waggy Avenue!

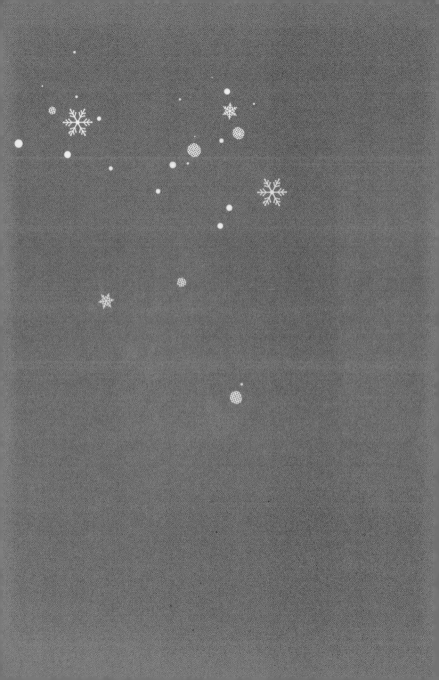

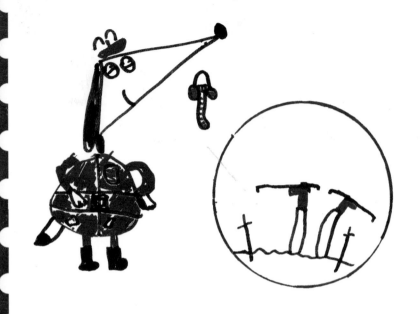

I like reading about Claude's super
adventures as he always saves the
day. Sir Bobblysock makes me
laugh. He always stops for cake!

By Abigail, Age 6